THIS WALKER BOOK BELONGS TO:

katie saxon

Book to read
to my class
at the end of the
day

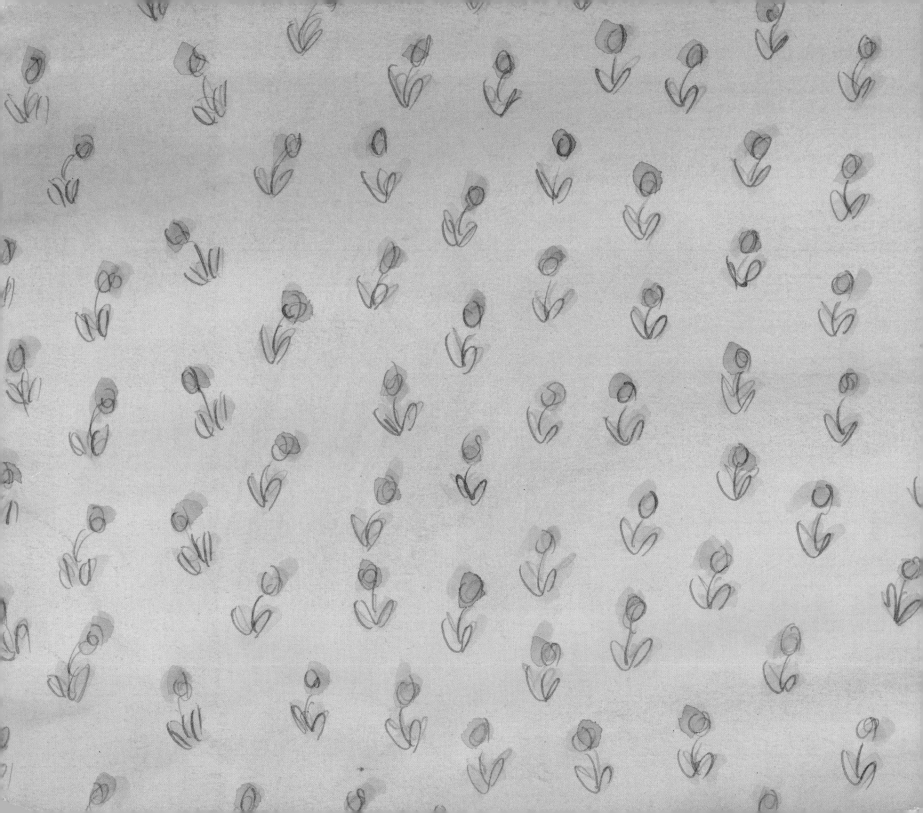

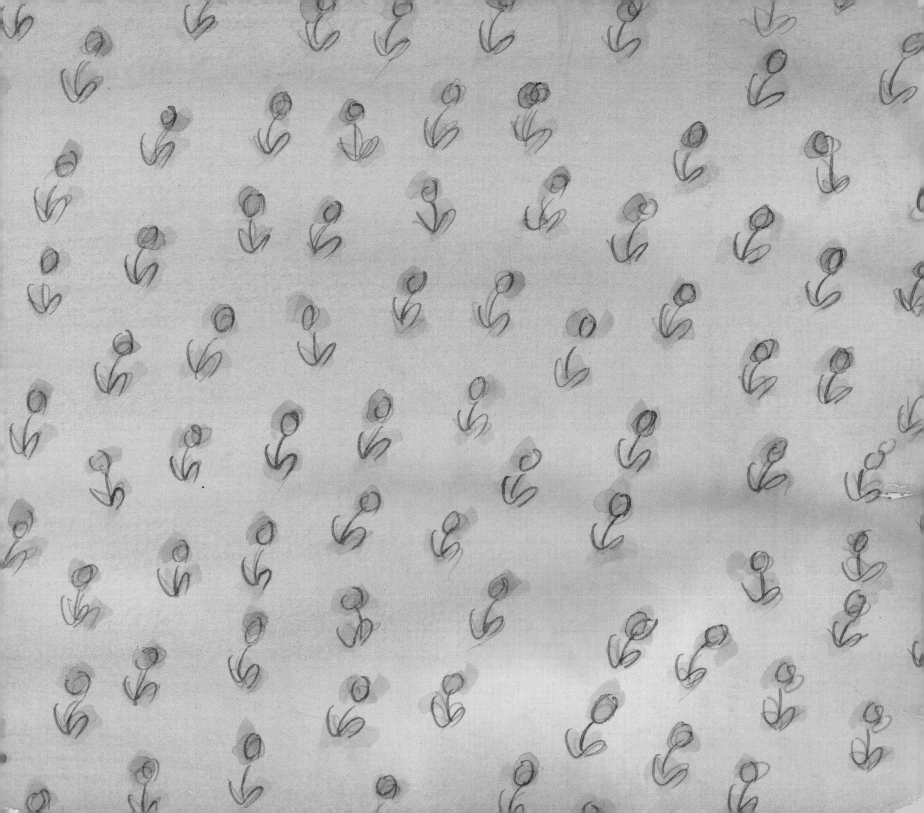

For my friend, Rachel Oscar
Love, Amy

For Anne Moore
Love, Christine

First published 2000 by Walker Books Ltd
87 Vauxhall Walk, London SE11 5HJ

This edition published 2001

2 4 6 8 10 9 7 5 3 1

Text © 2000 Amy Hest
Illustrations © 2000 Christine Davenier

This book has been typeset in Colwell Extra Light

Printed in Hong Kong

British Library Cataloguing in Publication Data:
a catalogue record for this book
is available from the British Library

ISBN 0-7445-7889-2

Mabel Dancing

Written by

Amy Hest

Illustrated by

Christine Davenier

WALKER BOOKS
AND SUBSIDIARIES
LONDON · BOSTON · SYDNEY

On the night of the dancing party, Mabel

blew bubbles in the bath while Mama dressed up

and Papa laced his dancing shoes. Mama blew kisses

and Papa did too, singing a song for Mabel.

"Shall we dance ...

shall we dance ...

shall we dance?"

When the bubbles were gone, Mabel wrapped herself in towels. Then she buttoned Mama's dressing-gown and it draped to the floor. She put her feet in Papa's velvet slippers that were green and she put her nose to the mirror.

"I can dance," Mabel said, and Curly Dog barked.

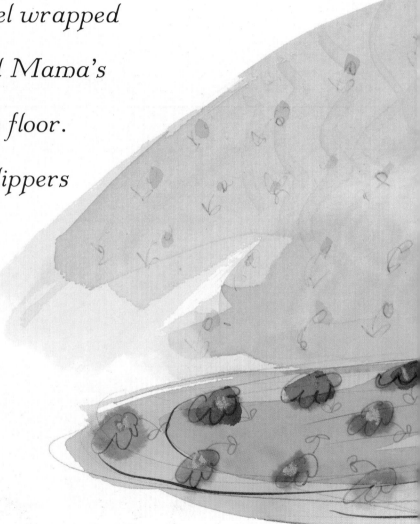

On the night of the dancing party,

Mabel was put to bed before the guests arrived,

and Mama tucked her in while Papa closed the

curtains. Then Papa tucked her in, and the

curtain blew and Mama's dress did, too.

"Sleep tight," they said.

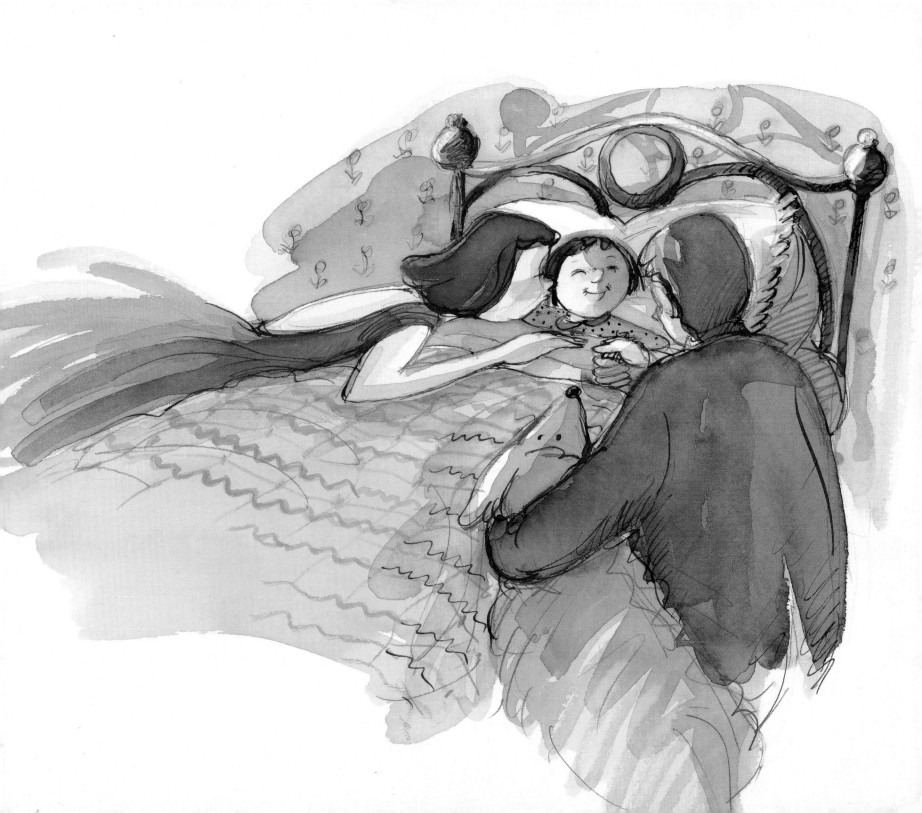

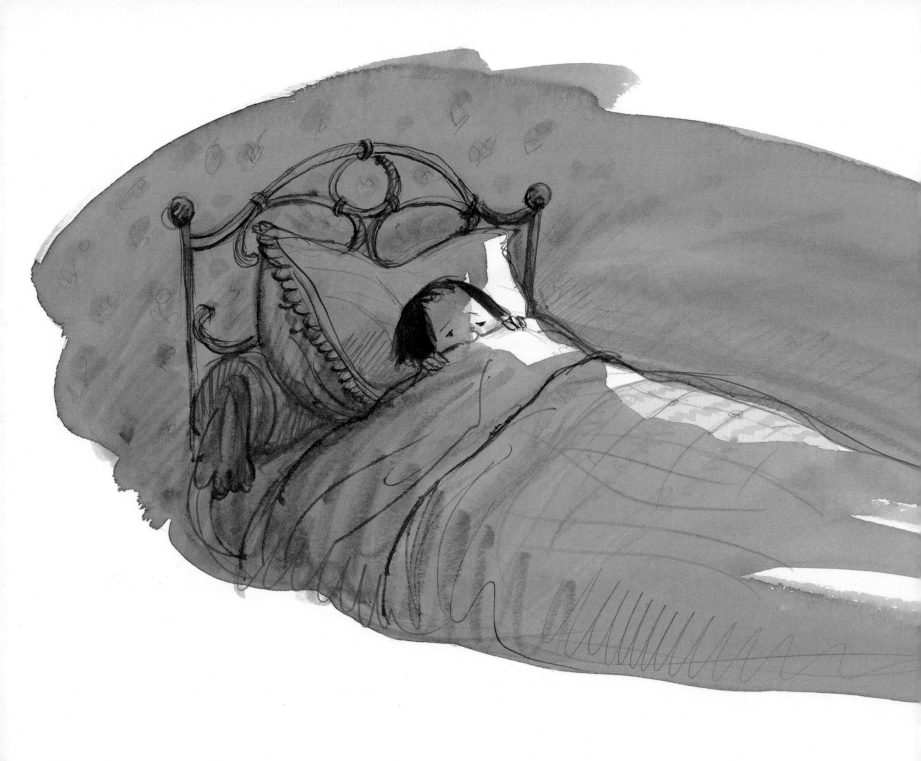

And there was Mabel, alone in the night.

From way down the stairs there was
music in the night and the music
had a way of floating up the stairs,
⌐ one, two, three ⌐
⌐ one, two, three ⌐
up and up the stairs.

Mabel hopped off the bed, hopping barefoot

to the window. Curly Dog came too, and

they stood by the glass, admiring the stars.

They counted Mabel's toes

and there were ten.

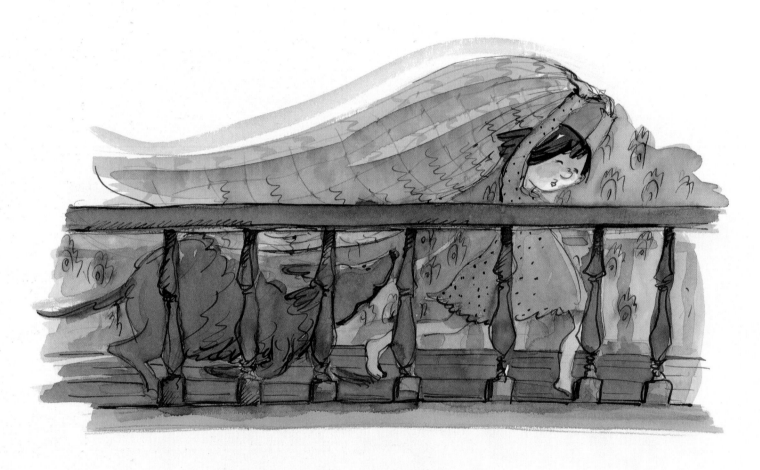

Mabel slid barefoot to the top of the stairs.

Curly Dog came too.

They sat down
and lay down
on Mabel's
yellow blanket.

From way down the stairs there was music

in the night, and papas in bow ties. Mamas

too, in swirling dresses, and the swirling

had a way of swooshing up the stairs,

⁓ swirl, two, three ⁓

⁓ swoosh, two, three ⁓

up and up the stairs.

"You dance," Mabel said.

Curly Dog yawned instead,

thumping his tail on the blanket.

Then Mabel stood up.

"Watch me!" she said, and off she went,

⌢ one, two, three ⌣

⌢ one, two, three ⌣

dancing down the stairs,

and she didn't make a sound,

⌢ shhh, two, three ⌣

⌢ shhh, two, three ⌣

down and down the stairs.

Mabel twirled and jumped in the bright party light and her blanket blew up like a yellow cape in the wind, making swirls.

And Mabel had a way of

spinning past the guests,

~ spin, two, three ~

— spin, two, three —

floating through the rooms.

Mama and Papa loved the show, and so did

the guests. Mabel bowed in her red nightdress.

"Shall we dance?" Papa said,
and they all danced away
in the velvet light.

Mama's dress swooshed and Papa's bow tie

tickled and they danced up the stairs,

⌒ one, two, three ⌒

⌒ one, two, three ⌒

up and up the stairs, with Mabel blowing kisses.

On the night of the dancing party, Mabel snuggled way down deep in the big blue bed.

Curly Dog snuggled too. Mabel closed her eyes, and the curtain blew like a yellow cape in the wind, making soft yellow swirls.

And from way down the stairs ...

the music played on,

~ one, two, three ~

~ one, two, three ~

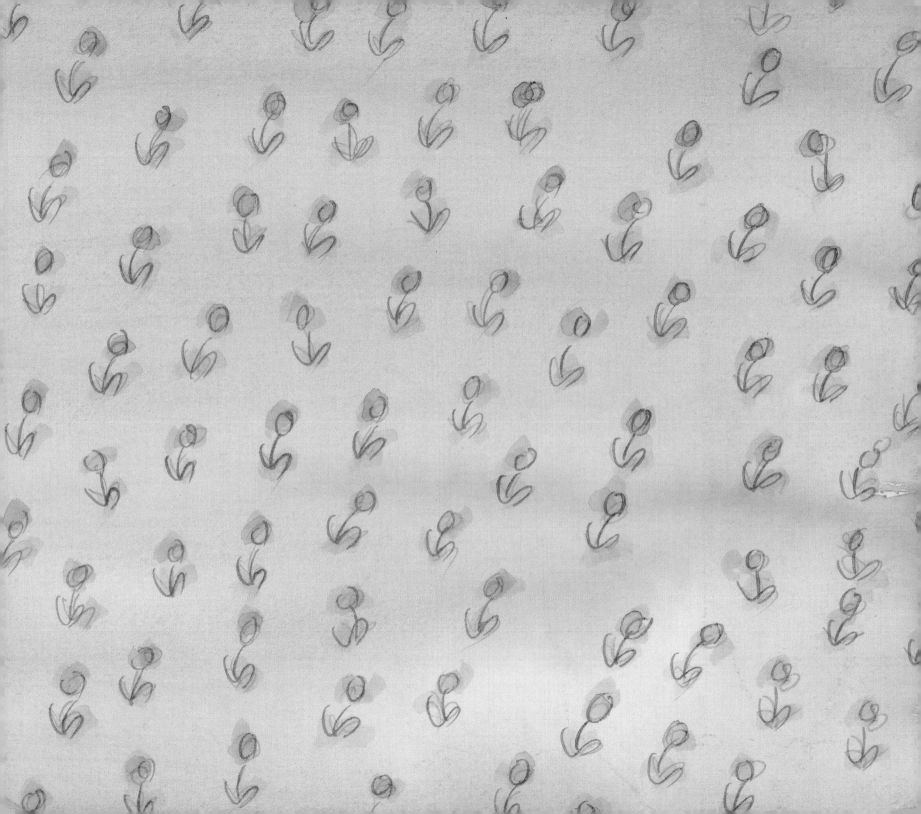

AMY HEST says of **Mabel Dancing**, "As a child, I longed to be invited to those exotic grown-up parties. I guess my grown-ups just forgot."

She is the author of many widely acclaimed books for children, including *When Jessie Came Across the Sea*, which won the prestigious Kate Greenaway Medal in 1998. Among her other books for Walker are *Rosie's Fishing Trip*; *Jamaica Louise James* and four Baby Duck books, *Baby Duck and the New Eyeglasses*; *In the Rain with Baby Duck*; *Off to School, Baby Duck* and *You're the Boss, Baby Duck*! Amy is married with two children, and lives in New York.

CHRISTINE DAVENIER also identifies strongly with Mabel's story. She says, "I think we all share with Mabel memories from our childhood of hiding in the dark, on the staircase, curious about what is going on in the 'adult world'. "

Christine has illustrated several books for children, including *Very Best (Almost) Friends: Poems of Friendship*, collected by Paul B. Janeczko, and her own stories *Frankie and Albertine* and *Sleepy Sophie*, all published by Walker.

Her happy memories of her childhood in France include spending time with her grandmother, a painter, and with her older sister, a passionate storyteller. It was in this creative environment that Christine decided to pursue a career in illustration. Christine lives in Paris with her daughter, Josephine.

Other Walker paperbacks

When Jessie Came Across the Sea by Amy Hest, illustrated by P.J. Lynch   0-7445-6963-X (p/b) £5.99

Rosie's Fishing Trip by Amy Hest, illustrated by Paul Howard   0-7445-4703-2 (p/b) £4.99

Frankie and Albertine by Christine Davenier   0-7445-7731-4 (p/b) £4.99

Sleepy Sophie by Christine Davenier   0-7445-7860-4 (p/b) £4.99